nightjar

nightjar

KATYA BALEN

Illustrated by
Richard Johnson

Barrington Stoke

First published in 2023 in Great Britain by
Barrington Stoke Ltd
18 Walker Street, Edinburgh, EH3 7LP

www.barringtonstoke.co.uk

Text © 2023 Katya Balen
Illustrations © 2023 Richard Johnson

A CIP catalogue record for this book is available
from the British Library upon request

ISBN: 978-1-80090-166-7

Printed in Great Britain by Charlesworth Press

To Sara Halter – for friendship, bad TV, bagels and hippos. You are the very best.

Chapter 1

I wake up in the pink light of early morning.
For a moment I'm not sure why my eyes are
open. There's a trilling in my ears and in a
dream-haze I panic. Has the tiny sparrow
tucked away in a cosy shoebox in the bottom
of my wardrobe escaped?

The sleepiness trickles out of me like sand
in a timer. I rub my eyes and I remember my
best friend Annie and I released the bird last
week. It was just before she went away for a
few weeks of summer music camp.

1

The trilling gets louder and louder.

I sit up and I see the soft glow of my mobile phone. The screen is flashing:

Dad calling
Dad calling
Dad calling

And the birdsong ringtone is fluttering around the room.

I can almost imagine it's spilling from the beaks of the birds on my wall. There are charcoal sketches swept in dusty lines on white

2

paper. All the birds I've ever seen. One day my whole room will be papered with them and the dull magnolia walls will disappear completely behind a sea of feathers and talons.

Dad calling
Dad calling
Dad calling

It must be midnight in New York but Dad is always up late. He likes to watch sports games he's recorded on his massive TV and catch up on emails and eat takeout noodles in the dark quiet of his apartment.

I've never actually been to his apartment but he sends me pictures sometimes. When he first moved in, he video-called me and carried his phone into every room so I could see the whole life he'd bought without me and Mum.

You have to call it an apartment because it's in America, but also because it's different to my flat in about a million ways. It has huge glass

windows and a view of the park. Dad says it's
very important to have a view of the park if you
live in New York.

I once asked him what birds he could see in
the park and from his windows that frame the
whole sky. He just looked blankly at me from
the computer screen and said something about
pigeons.

Dad calling
Dad calling
Dad calling

I can see blackbirds and crows and starlings and
finches and sparrows and gulls and a thousand
others from my small square window in my
little flat. Once, I was watching for a nightjar
because they're strange and beautiful and full
of myths and secrets. Instead, I saw the wings
of an owl beat in the stardusted night air and it
was magic.

So I don't mind that Dad has a huge TV and a view of the park and a new girlfriend called Georgia and an apartment three thousand miles away and a job that means he can only come and see me once a year. I've got everything I need right here. Just me and Mum and Annie and the birds. The ones I've seen and the ones I will see.

Dad calling
Dad calling
Dad calling

I turn my phone over so the insistent message is shouting into my pillow. I roll over and I try to go back to sleep just as the daybirds start to sing.

Chapter 2

Later that morning I'm eating breakfast as fast as I possibly can without choking on toast and honey.

I could be as slow as I like because it's the summer holidays but I want to go out and try to spot the woodpecker I know I heard yesterday. It was tapping its beak in a tree in the park and the sound bounced into the clouds. So I'm matching my bites of toast to the fast *click click click* of Mum's sewing machine.

The needle is flickering up and down like a silver fish darting into the waves of white fabric. Mum's making a tiny lace gown and it's going to be beautiful but it's also very terrible because whenever Mum makes those gowns it's not for a baby that's alive.

She says it's an honour and a privilege to make them but I just think it's sad. Those little white gowns hang like ghosts in our flat until Mum delivers them to the hospital wrapped in careful layers of soft tissue paper.

Mum's phone pings and she pauses the next tiny stitch to check it. I can tell by the way her eyebrows pull tight together that the email is from Dad. I think of the missed calls from earlier and my phone still buried under my pillow.

"It's from your dad," Mum says, but I already knew that. Her eyes scan down the blocks of text. There's a lot of it. Dad normally sends one line, like:

Happy birthday!
Well done, champ!
Georgia and I bought a kitten – see pic!

Dad doesn't have a lot to say to us but that's OK. I never really know what to say to him either.

Mum scrolls down the email and the line of her eyebrows tightens like a knot of wool. I have the same tightness but it's in my chest. I am suddenly nervous and I try to guess what he's saying.

Maybe Dad and Georgia broke up. Maybe the kitten is sick again. It had some stomach bug and he sent me a longer-than-normal message about how they'd got in one of those yellow New York cabs to rush it to the vet. The kitten was wrapped in a blanket and the driver took them to the hospital because he thought they were talking about their baby being sick.

Maybe Dad's fancy new apartment burned down. Maybe his baseball team lost. He never really never tells me much, so my mind whizzes through the possibilities from tiny to huge and back again.

Mum looks up from her phone.

"He says he's coming to the UK," she tells me.

I wouldn't have ever guessed that in a million years.

Dad always comes in the winter. I can only imagine him dressed in his dove-grey soft wool coat and cashmere scarf, standing in the dull pale light of December skies. He comes and lights Chanukah candles with us and eats the doughnuts Mum makes. He always gives me a present that's expensive and which he thinks I'll love.

My wardrobe is heaving with baseball caps and T-shirts that tell me I love NY. There are stiff leather mitts for catching balls and oversized American football shirts and fancy trainers that you can't get dirty.

I once told Dad what I really wanted was a new pair of binoculars and he laughed so loud he scared the birds from the trees. He said I was a *card*, whatever that means. He told me that people in New York queued for hours for the high-top trainers he'd just given me and they were limited edition.

"Dad says he's coming to your Bar Mitzvah," Mum adds. Her eyebrows are disappearing up into her hairline now. My mouth hangs open.

A lump of honeyed toast falls out of my mouth.
It lands on the table with a wet and sticky
thump.

"I didn't know you'd invited him," I say, and
I swipe at the honey mush on the tablecloth.
A damp crumb flies close to the sad and
beautiful gown rippling like a foamy wave in
Mum's sewing machine. She flinches but she
doesn't tell me off.

"He's your father, Noah," she says. "I know he's far away and I know you don't really see eye to eye, but I was worried you'd regret not having him there. It's an important day."

"I should have had a choice," I say. "It's the day I become responsible for *myself*. It's the day my actions are my own and not my parents'."

I stop there and I let the words hang in the toasted air of the kitchen. I don't say the next bit because Mum already knows.

Dad has never been responsible for me.

chapter 3

Dad's plane lands in the UK one whole week before my Bar Mitzvah. I thought maybe he'd fly overnight and land in the early morning of the day itself. I thought he'd dash back across the ocean in time for dinner and work again the next morning. I thought I'd just have to shake Dad's hand and hear his congratulations and then he'd slip back into his life and I'd slip back into mine.

But Dad's here for a week and he's waiting on the doorstep to take me for a drive. I don't think that really counts as an actual activity, especially not here. The city streets are clogged and dirty and cars crawl like limp beetles in the summer heat.

Dad landed at 8 a.m. and he's driven straight to our flat in a huge black car that he's rented. It shines bright in the early morning sun and I have to shield my eyes.

Dad swings himself down from the driver's seat and his shape looms and twists and pulls into sharp focus in front of me. I always forget how tall he is. He unfolds himself as he gets out of the car and it's like he could reach up a hand and pluck the sun from the sky.

"All right, champ?" says Dad, and his vowels are all stretched and strange and American. When he lived here, his voice softened into English sounds but since he's moved back it's changed again.

"Hi, Dad," I say, and the words taste unfamiliar.

I try to remember the last time I saw him. Dad didn't come last winter. He was planning on it but something happened at work or with

Georgia or with Georgia's kid, whose name rolls around at the back of my brain but I can't quite catch hold of it.

I can't remember why he didn't come. He sent me a huge box of sticky and sharp American candy, I remember that. Annie and I spent a day turning our tongues different colours of the rainbow as we ate it. We spat the sugar shards into the bin when we got ones that tasted like grape.

"Shall we get going then?" Dad goes on. "I thought we could drive out into the country. You like that sort of thing, right? And I could do with blasting away some of the old jetlag cobwebs."

"Great," I say. I'm surprised because I didn't think Dad would think about what I might like to do. I thought we'd be stuck in an endless loop of the city streets, sitting in the car not looking at each other and listening to terrible pop music instead of using our own words.

I haul myself into the front seat. I feel like I do when I go up to the roof of our block of flats to watch the sky for birds and stars. I'm so high up that it's weird.

Mum gives Dad a hug hello and goodbye because they don't hate each other like some parents do when they split up. They're just far apart. Then Mum leans in through the window. She gives me a kiss on the cheek and a package wrapped in brown paper which I know will be something baked and delicious. Dad gets back in the car and sniffs the bag approvingly.

"Have fun, guys!" Mum says in a cheery voice that sounds like plastic. Fake and bright.

Dad raises a hand in mock salute and sweeps the huge car along the street and out of the city.

Chapter 4

The city fades away and the world turns green around us. We sit in silence.

I watch the trees spread their branches brushed with shades of lime and jade and emerald. The sky is the kind of burnt blue that only happens when the day is going to be scorching hot. I can almost taste the heat in the air as I look out for the dip of a swallow's tail or the sweep of a kestrel's wing.

I won't see a nightjar because, as the name says, they like the dusk and the dark. But as we drive further and further into the countryside I do feel a spill of excitement despite being here with Dad. It's strange and uncomfortable and not what either of us really wants.

"So, is school good?" says Dad finally.

I guess the silence got too much for him. He doesn't like the quiet. When he calls me, he always tries to fill it with so many words that my head spins and I can't find the end of one of his sentences and the beginning of another.

"Yeah, it's OK," I say. I'm craning my neck because I'm sure I might have just spotted the shadow of a goshawk brushing the clouds.

"Have you learned your Torah reading for the big day?" Dad says, and he fiddles with the radio. Pop music beats through the silence because I'm distracted by the world outside the windows and don't answer.

"Noah?" Dad says.

"What?" I ask. "Oh, yeah. Maybe. Not sure." I don't really want to talk to him about my Bar Mitzvah. Of course I've already learned the reading. I've been practising for months, the strange and beautiful syllables of Hebrew threading through me like a song.

"Exciting though, isn't it?" Dad says. "Becoming a man?"

"Yeah, it'll be good," I say flatly. I know he's trying but it's so hard. I don't think about my Bar Mitzvah like that – becoming a man. I think about being thoughtful and careful and responsible. I'm not sure that's what Dad means.

"Try out for any sports teams?" Dad tries. He is really trying. He just keeps getting it wrong.

The light is flickering through the windows and I can't see the shape of the goshawk in the sky any more. I buzz the window down

and stick my head out. A hot stream of air
rushes through my hair and my ears are filled
with the roar of a lorry passing on the other
side of the road. It blares its horn and I see
a branch overhanging the road just in time.
I jump backwards in my seat before the tree
can swipe me.

"Jesus, Noah, what the hell are you playing
at?" Dad shouts, and the car weaves as Dad
trembles with shock.

"Saw a bird," I mutter. I stare at my boots
as they flake mud on the perfect dark of the
car's carpet. My heart thumps fast and heavy
in my chest from the shock and the metal flash
of the lorry and for the missed moment of
goshawk.

"You and your bloody birds," says Dad. "I
thought you might have grown up and out of
that by now."

I feel like a little kid. Tiny in the huge car and the huge green world.

When I look up, the sky is empty and Dad is staring straight at the road ahead.

Chapter 5

Dad parks the car in a tiny empty car park at the side of a flat field edged with trees. The car takes up two spaces carefully chalked in white on the ground, but there's no one here to complain.

I slither down from my seat and Dad locks the door with a clunk. He grabs a brand-new backpack from the boot and changes his bright white trainers for walking boots. They still have their tags on.

"Do you need to …?" Dad asks, gesturing at my feet, but I'm wearing my boots because I'm always wearing my boots. "Oh great, you came prepared. Me too! I've got water, snack bars and waterproofs." He looks up at the burning blue sky. "Can't hurt, right?"

"Sure," I say. "Let's walk."

I put my binoculars round my neck but the thing Dad said about growing up and being too old for birds is still burning in my ears. So I don't lift them to the sky even though I'm sure I saw the low circling flight of a young red kite hovering with spread wings over the field.

I squint into the sun but I can't make anything out. I've never seen a red kite in real life before. Birds of prey don't tend to circle above cities. If I see one, I could sketch it for my wall. I imagine my charcoal dusting the fork of a red kite's tail and the sharp curve of its beak.

"Come on, kiddo!" says Dad. He's charging towards the stile to get into the field. This isn't going to be a walk; it's going to be a race. I want to go slowly and I want to look at every little thing. I want to listen to birdsong that isn't accompanied by the roar of traffic and the swirl of city noise.

But Dad is already disappearing into the tall green grass.

Chapter 6

Dad walks twice as fast as I thought was even possible. He isn't out of breath but there's a pearly shine of sweat on his forehead. I slow down sometimes to touch the fronds of a fern or peer into a tree to see a featherflap burst of wings beating the air, but every time, Dad says something like, "Come on, kiddo," or "We'll never do the whole walk at this rate."

I hear the echoing knock of a woodpecker but I still don't get to see one. I watch the flame wings of a kite spiralling through the air towards something unseen. I see the blue-black inky feathers of crows scattering as a kestrel swoops.

I stop caring about Dad rolling his eyes and telling me to hurry up and I look into my binoculars and I see the world around me.

Dad gives up and marches ahead after a while. I hear the *clomp clomp clomp* of his boots and the swish of air moving past him. It is so strange seeing him in the bright British sun and not in the blue glass of my phone. He trails his hand along a bush and his thumbs brush the leaves so gently that for a moment my heart

squeezes. Under this huge sky Dad looks so small. He looks lonely.

I run after him to catch up.

He's not looking where he's putting his feet in his brand-new walking boots with their stiff and shining leather. So I see it first. I don't think Dad would have seen it at all. There would have been a sickening *snap-crunch* of bird bones and skull and the crush of heavy boots.

"Stop!" I shout wildly, and I wave my arms despite being behind him. "Stop! Don't put your foot down!"

Dad actually listens and he stops with his foot hovering in mid-air, balancing on one leg like a wobbly heron.

I run forward and dive to the ground with Dad's confused face above me. I make my hands into a careful cage around the ball of frightened feathers.

"What on earth are you doing?" says Dad,
and he plants his foot on the other side of my
head. "What is that?"

I shift my body so the sunlight brightens the
bird and I show Dad the shaking puff he nearly
stamped out. Its feathers are patterned like

bark and its wide mouth opens and closes in silent terror.

"What is that?" Dad says again.

"It's a nightjar," I say, and I'm breathless, so the words whoosh out as soft as clouds.

Nightjars are beautiful and magical and rare and I can't believe there's one right here next to me. It's like something from a dream. I long to reach out and touch its bark feathers with my fingertips but I know I can't.

"It shouldn't be awake now," I say. "There must be something wrong." I crouch closer to the nightjar and I try not to startle it or get too close because I know that will upset it. Nightjars nest on the ground but I think from its balding patches of feathers that it has parasites. Just like the sparrow Annie and I released last week.

Dad looks down at me and the handful of nightjar and there is confusion scribbled across his unfamiliar face. I don't know him well enough to know what he's thinking.

"Right," he says. "Well, there's not a lot we can do about it, is there?" He shrugs his big shoulders. "Sad, but that's nature, right? That's what happens. It'll make a good snack for a lucky fox."

Dad's words are as sharp as spears. I know he doesn't mean to sound so harsh but I feel the words bite anyway.

"No," I say. "Not this one. Because I can help. Annie and I do it all the time."

"Annie?" Dad's face cracks open into a grin. "That your girlfriend? Good on you, kiddo."

"No," I say again, but there's no point because however I say it he won't believe me. He'll start saying how *cute* it is that I deny it. So I change direction. "I can help the bird. We need to go back to the car and go home. I have everything at home. We have to take it home."

Dad laughs.

"Noah, you can't be serious. It's a bird. There are a million of them. More. This is what happens. You should know that more than anyone. They get caught or they get sick and they die."

"Not this one," I say. "I found it. So now it can have another chance. Can I please have your waterproof jacket? I can carry the bird in it and keep it cosy and in the dark."

Dad stares at me, huge again. He's six feet tall and all the way above me.

"Noah, we're on a walk," Dad says. "Out in nature, like you love. Sky and trees full of birds. And now you're saying you want to interfere in the natural way of things, and you also want to leave and go home?"

I stare back at him and I don't blink as I reply, "Exactly."

Dad shoves his hands deep into his pockets until the seams crack. He blows out air into the summer day. He rolls his eyes up to the summer sky.

I stay crouched on the ground with the nightjar blinking slowly in the unfamiliar daylight.

"Come on, Noah," Dad says. There is a muscle flickering in his jaw. "This is ridiculous. You can't save the bird. The bird will either save itself or it will die. That's nature. That's the way things go sometimes."

Fury swirls like a tornado in my chest. I take deep breaths. I hardly ever get cross. But I hardly ever talk to Dad.

"If it's just the way things go, then why do we ever interfere?" I ask. "Why do we help people when they're ill or hurt? Why did you take Buttons to the vet?"

"That's different." Dad's hands move from his pockets and he puts them on his hips. His fingers are rippling across the fabric. His toes tap.

"Why?" I say. "You wanted to help her and you could help her, so you did."

"Buttons isn't a wild animal," Dad replies. "She's a purebred ragdoll kitten and Georgia and I love her. We weren't about to let her die in pain. She's our pet. She trusts us. We knew we could help her. This bird is just scared."

I pause because he's right and the bird is scared. But scared is better than dead. I can help. I can help. I know I can. I stay crouched on the ground.

"I'm being responsible," I say. "For myself and for the bird." I let the word "responsible" out of my mouth slowly and carefully.

Dad rolls his eyes to the sky again.

"I don't think that's quite right," he says very quietly, but he takes off his backpack and he gives me his shiny new waterproof jacket. His mouth is set in a line as wide as the nightjar's gasping beak.

Chapter 7

The silence in the car on the way home is as sharp as glass. Dad puts the radio on but I turn it down so low that the songs are a whisper and then Dad turns it off. Air rushes by us and the countryside twists and fades into city streets.

The nightjar is in a shoebox, the one from Dad's new walking boots. I carried its tiny quivering body back to the car in a sling made from his waterproof jacket.

Dad wasn't happy about using the jacket or the shoebox and he keeps saying things about how much car-rental companies charge for soiled interiors. I don't think he'll want his jacket back.

When we get to my block of flats, I hop out and grab the shoebox before Dad can make me throw it in a bin or something. I streak past the lift because it's broken and I take the stairs two at a time until I can burst through our front door.

Mum is braiding challah in the kitchen. She flicks thin ropes of dough over and under and round in a magic of movement that I can never do.

"Noah?" Mum says. "You're back early! Where's your dad? What's in the box? Another bird?"

I nod because Mum doesn't mind my birds. She names them even when I don't because if you name them, it's harder to let them go.

Dad's right in one way. They're not pets. They're wild and they should be free and I'll help them get there. I give Mum a smile because I don't want her to worry about me and Dad. Then I go into my bedroom without answering her other questions.

I shut the door firmly behind me and sit on the floor. As carefully as I can, I transfer the nightjar from the shoebox to my birdbox. My birdbox is actually just a shoebox with holes in the top but it's a nice size and it's cosy and dark.

I'm careful not to touch the nightjar and it peers up at me with furious eyes. I scatter mealworms in at its clawed feet and then I close the box because the dark will keep it calm.

I can hear Dad's voice in the kitchen. It is low and rumbling. I search under my bed for my box of bird supplies. They are neatly divided and labelled in a fishing-tackle box. There are paintbrushes and sachets of cat food and water droppers and parasite treatments and scraps of material for bedding.

I check the label on the parasite treatment and I lift open the lid of the birdbox just a bit so I can take a picture with my phone. The nightjar blinks in the flood of light and it's so beautiful that my heart fizzes. But I close the box and leave it in peace as I text Ben the vet and attach the picture.

Two minutes later the voices in the kitchen are still low and rumbling when my phone trills with a message:

*Good plan, let me know if you need help but
I'm sure you have it under control as always.
See you Saturday! Ben*

The front door shuts and the flat is silent.

Chapter 8

I keep the nightjar fed and watered. It makes a peeping sound when the sun goes down and I open the box to let it taste the night air on its beak. The nightjar stretches its speckled wings and it gapes its wide mouth. I draw its lines in charcoal and I study its shape and the way it turns its head and the way it shuffles low to the ground.

I read about how nightjars are written about in mythology. They are linked to night and

darkness and death. Some people think they're a curse.

My nightjar is beautiful.

In the low light it looks like a patch of night sky. Its feathers are swirled with constellations. A map of its world is patterned onto its wings.

Mum comes into my room the day after I found the bird. She sits on my bed while I try to make the speckled feathers come alive in my sketchbook.

"Your dad should have been more supportive, I know that, Noah," Mum says, and I know there's something coming next and that I won't like it much.

"But you need to meet him halfway. Or even quarter way. I know it's not great. I know the distance is hard and I know you don't think you're very alike. And maybe you're not. But you have to try a bit. Talk to him properly."

I open my mouth to interrupt but Mum holds up a hand to stop me. Her fingertips are red from the rub of fabric running through her machine over and over and over again.

"I know he has to try too!" she says. "I've told him that. But every time he tries to talk to you, you clam up. It's not easy to break into your shell sometimes." She raps her knuckles on my head like I'm a shell fresh out of the ocean. "When your dad asks you something, try and say more than one word? Just try. Please?"

I think about my one-word answers in the car and the stomp of my boots on the walk and my silent fury when Dad didn't want me to scoop up the bird.

"OK," I say.

*

That evening Dad comes and he takes me to dinner. Mum stays behind to sew more sad gowns. I would much rather stay and help her find tiny buttons and stitch sprays of stars into the folds of soft fabric. But I have to try.

When Dad arrives, everything is stiff and formal. I move differently and so does he. We stand far apart and he asks about my day. I say it was good and then I ask about his day and he says he went to London for work and it was good too.

We get in the huge car and we drive to a pizza place that we definitely could have walked to instead. I watch the daylight misting into night and the streetlights streaming in orange orbs past the window.

We get seated and I get a lemonade and Dad gets a beer, then we spend ages looking at the menu instead of talking to each other even though I already know I want the Veggie Special with extra onions. Dad orders a Meat

Feast. I know he eats things I don't eat like pork and prawns but I wish he didn't have to do it right now.

"You know," he says, his mouth full of pizza. "I found an injured fox cub when I was about your age. Dogs had been at it. Great chunks taken out of it." He chews a piece of pepperoni and I smell meat.

"Yeah?" I say carefully. "What happened?"

"The fox was screaming," he says. The pepperoni is spicing the air and it burns my nostrils. "I did what I had to do."

I feel icicles start to spike in my blood.

"What did you have to do?" I whisper. I haven't eaten any of my pizza. The mushrooms are hardening into slug slime. I pick up a piece just to have something to do with my hands. The cheese stretches thin and tight as I pull the slice from the plate.

"I put it out of its misery," Dad says. "With a rock. Quickly. Jesus, Noah, don't look at me like that. It was the kindest thing to do. The fox was in agony. It wasn't going to survive."

"You don't know that!" I say, and my voice rises above the clatter of plates and the noise of families having fun. "You could have helped it! You killed it!"

Dad puts down his pizza slice. A greasy piece of pepper snakes its way onto his plate.

"Noah, I told you that story because I wanted you to know that I didn't tell you to leave the bird because I'm evil or cruel or whatever you think I am. It was the responsible thing to do."

"It wasn't responsible!" I say, and a few people turn to look.

"Noah, you're not even thirteen yet," Dad says. "You don't know how things work. You get furious with me for not doing what you'd do, but you haven't tried to understand why I did it. I did what was kindest for that fox. And I think it would have been kinder to leave that bird where it was rather than stress it out and put it in a box and treat it when it doesn't have a clue what's going on."

"*You* don't have a clue what's going on," I say. "You don't know me at all. You don't know what I like or what I do. You never listen to me. You don't know how many birds I've saved or how much it matters to them and to me. You don't understand me. You don't know what I like to do. You don't know anything at all. You say what you would do and what you think and what the best way to do something is. You never stop for one moment to think about me. Who I am. What I want. How I work. You never ask a single thing that matters and you don't care about the answers anyway."

There's a long silence. I put down my pizza slice with trembling fingers and I get up and I walk out. I walk the city streets home and it takes ten minutes and I see a cloud of summer starlings flying low.

Chapter 9

Mum isn't very happy with me when I come home and I'm alone and I'm starving because I haven't had any supper. She gives me fresh soup with the challah she made yesterday. I spread the twisted bread with a thick layer of salt-studded butter and I dip it into the spicy tomato soup and it tastes incredible.

"What happened?" Mum asks. She's ironing a tiny sad dress and reading a pattern for a wedding dress at the same time. Mum twists different strands of life together just like she plaits challah.

"Dad killed a fox," I say shortly.

Mum looks up through a cloud of iron steam.

"Yes," she says. "He did."

"You knew?" I say. "You knew Dad murdered an innocent animal and you didn't think you should mention it to me?"

"Noah, calm down," Mum says. "Did he tell you why?"

"Yeah," I say. My pulse is bouncing in my ears. "He should have helped it."

"He couldn't help it," Mum replies. "He was in the middle of nowhere, on a hike somewhere in the Catskills. He was miles from phone reception, miles from a vet, no car anywhere near. What would you have done?"

"Carried it," I say stubbornly. "What was Dad doing on a hike anyway?"

"He used to love that sort of thing," Mum says. "Loved it. He said hiking made him feel like he was alive and like he was part of a world that was old and new all at once."

"That's ridiculous," I mutter. "If he cared about the world, he'd have carried the fox. I would have."

"That would have hurt it," Mum says softly. "Carrying it would have frightened it beyond anything I can describe. Who would you be doing that for? You, or the fox?"

I swallow the last of my soup and I don't answer her. I go to my bedroom and I go to my nightjar.

Chapter 10

For the next few days I practise my Torah reading. I don't leave my room very much except to sit and watch murmurations of starlings practising their shape in the sky over the park.

I know Mum and Dad speak on the phone because I hear the low burr of her voice seeping under my door. But I can't catch what she's saying and I don't really care. Dad doesn't come round and Mum doesn't mention him.

I say the words of my Torah reading like a spell until they take on new life and new meaning and I hear them in new ways. The rise and fall of Hebrew soothes me like a wave. I read to the nightjar in its darkened box. I whisper the syllables and I hope the song of my words makes it feel safe. I feel a twinge of nerves every time I think about saying them to anyone but the bird.

The parasite treatment seems to be working. It normally takes a few days and already the nightjar's feathers are shining brighter and it is starting to explore the dark corners of its box.

It is stronger now that it isn't fighting off the parasites. It eats the bugs I put in its box and it stretches its wings and remembers it can fly. I send new photos to Ben the vet and he replies with a thumbs-up emoji. I google the night-vision binoculars I've wanted for ever and I imagine using them to watch the nightjar swooping free towards the moon.

On Wednesday I let the nightjar out of its box. It hops and peeps and I stay very still. I can see its little heart beating hard in its puffed chest. It is so much more alive than before. It is nearly ready to go.

My bedroom lights are off and the curtains are pulled shut. There is only the dim glow of my bedside lamp, shining like a yellow moon. The nightjar hops slowly towards the light and flaps its stardust wings and I can see every ragged feather and every wrinkle on its curling feet.

I remember the stories about nightjars being full of black magic and cursed and cloaked in death. I wonder if the people who told those stories were just afraid of a nightjar's strangeness. A wide mouth that gapes and stretches in a pink yawn. Dark feathers on its head that twitch and tremble. Narrow beetle-black eyes. I find its strangeness beautiful.

I move to get my sketchpad because I want to draw it right now and record every single detail so that when it's gone back into the night sky I will remember. In a few days it will be gone for ever.

But my movement surprises the nightjar and it flaps and cries and shrinks away from me. It huddles in the corner of my bedroom far away from me and my heart twists.

It is so very frightened of the world I've given it.

It is so very frightened of me.

And I feel the question form in my mind before I can clamp down the steel doors of my brain and shut it off.

Did I save the nightjar for it or for me?

Chapter 11

I haven't heard from Dad and I haven't texted him either.

The week creeps on.

There's suit measuring and Torah practice and summer swallows and the knock of a woodpecker and the memories of the argument.

On Friday the nightjar is ready to go home.

There is one small issue.

It needs to be released at night and it needs to be released back where I found it. Far away from the city. Somewhere it can flap its wings and fold itself into darkness.

Mum and I don't have a car and the buses don't run that way and that late. I google over and over on my phone and the journey will take me eleven hours by foot. I consider it.

"Don't be ridiculous, Noah," Mum says. She's pinning a dress into place on a dummy and turning it from a sack into something sleek and new. "It's your Bar Mitzvah tomorrow. You're not walking forty miles the night before. You won't make it back in time for one thing, and your feet will probably fall off. I've measured you perfectly for your suit. I'm not making adjustments now."

But the nightjar has to go home.

Mum is looking at me. She has dress pins in her mouth and a look on her face that means *You know what to do, Noah.*

So I text the one person I know with a car and the one person who knows exactly where we need to go.

Chapter 12

The knock at the front door startles both of us. Mum goes to open it and in a rush of aftershave there is Dad. He's carrying a holdall and also a fat paper bag and I wonder what he's brought me this time. A silky sports jacket or an American football or a book about baseball probably.

He holds the paper bag out to me.

It's stuffed with rugelach. Rugelach is my favourite thing in the whole world. It's a bit like tiny croissants stuffed with sticky chocolate goo.

But really that doesn't come close to describing how delicious it is.

I remember Chanukah when I was six and stuffing myself silly with it and being sick. Dad gently wiped the chocolate and puke off my face and told me when I was bigger and more grown up I'd know when to stop.

I open the bag and there are at least thirty pieces nestled in paper folds.

He reaches into his holdall and produces a cardboard box.

"I know presents are traditional on the day of your Bar Mitzvah," he says. "But I thought you might like this one a bit early. I thought it might help tonight." There's a crack of something in his voice. Hope?

I take the box. It's shiny and blue and there's no wrapping paper on it, so I can see what it is right away. Night-vision binoculars.

The exact ones I've been looking at online for months and months.

"Good for spotting owls too," Dad says. "I know it's not ... I know it's not enough, Noah. But it's a start, I hope."

"Thanks," I say quietly. I'm thinking about foxes and birds and nature and wildness and cruelty and kindness. I'm thinking of that funny strange space where people and things and actions can be wrong and right at the very same time.

Chapter 13

Dad and I drive into the night together. I am holding the box close to my chest. I can feel the bird inside, like shifting sand. Ready to go. Ready to be free and wild and haunt the night again.

We drive in silence. It feels like one of us is waiting for the other one to talk and no one knows how to start.

I watch the world turning ink-blue outside. The leaves shine with moonlight. By the time

Dad pulls into the tiny empty car park, the darkness is total.

I put on my head torch and I expect Dad to laugh but he says something about that being really sensible. He uses the torch on his phone and we walk together in the bright streams of blue and yellow light that shine from each of us.

We reach the right sort of spot. It's sheltered enough to feel safe and secure, but there's a clear view of the wide and wild world beyond. The nightjar can choose to slip into the shadows or take flight.

I crouch down and Dad does the same. He's right next to me in the darkness as I open the box. I tip it gently onto its side so the nightjar can just walk out.

It does just that. Slowly at first. Just a little rustling as its clawed feet scrabble against cardboard. I angle my headtorch up to the sky

so it isn't startled by the light, and Dad swipes
off his torch app. The moon glows blue.

The nightjar is cautious. It hops and stops.
It looks like it's tasting the air. Checking
this isn't a trick. Its feathers glitter in the
starlight. It becomes part of the darkness

and yet somehow its own thing too. I use my night-vision binoculars and the shape of the bird is now green. They're ace.

I look over at Dad. He's transfixed.

"It looks so different," he whispers quietly. I hope it's so the nightjar doesn't tremble. "So different. It's wonderful. What a thing."

"Nightjars are made for the night-time," I whisper back.

"Yes," says Dad. "It looks right. It looks like it belongs. But it's not just that. When we found it, it was half dead. It was dull. Its eyes … they'd given up. But now. It's transformed, Noah. You did that."

I shrug but I can feel my cheeks rushing red. I offer him the binoculars and he takes them.

"I'm sorry," says Dad. He looks through the lenses and into the dark. "You were right. I didn't listen. Not when we found the bird, and not before, and not after."

Those words feel so big even when there aren't many of them.

"I know why you did what you did," I say. "With the fox. I understand it now. It's all a balance. There's right and wrong and there's black and white and night and day and then sometimes it's all mixed up. I thought I knew which was which but now ... I'm not so sure."

"No," says Dad. "Neither am I. I think that's what growing up means. Knowing and not knowing. Noah, I'm so proud of you. I'm so proud of you for taking responsibility for this little life. I don't know if it will always be the right thing to do, or whether it would be wrong not to do it. But I trust you. I trust you to think and judge and grow. Because you're extraordinary. I don't think I knew quite how extraordinary."

I move my arms in a low and slow movement so I don't startle the exploring bird, and throw them around Dad.

And the nightjar flaps its wings and disappears into the star-filled sky.

Chapter 14

Mum has finished my suit for the Bar Mitzvah. It's deep navy blue. When I see it hanging dully in my wardrobe on Saturday morning, I feel a tiny swoop of disappointment because it's so boring. It looks like something you'd wear if you worked in an office on a computer. I put it on without paying any attention and run my hands through my hair to try to make my curls flatter but they explode as soon as I move my hand away.

I turn around in front of the mirror and there is a burst of colour from somewhere inside the folds of navy fabric.

Mum has lined the inside with flashes and scraps of silk and so when my jacket flaps open it looks like the wings of a bird. The suit transforms and it's brilliant. It's the best thing I have ever worn.

Mum comes into the room in her best dress. It is emerald green and she glows.

"Thank you," I whisper as I stare at my reflection. "It's perfect."

I look different. Older. Taller. More like the person I will be. Like the mirror is showing me a tiny shard of the future.

Mum smiles at me and her eyes are bright with tears.

"I used scraps from your grandparents' Bar and Bat Mitzvah outfits and your cousins' too, and mine, and your dad's." Mum says the last word firmly and she strokes the suit fabric. "Everyone with you all at once.

"My boy," Mum adds. "All grown up and altogether himself."

She puts her arm around me. I lean into her and breathe in the smell of fabric and safety pins and bread and her. My mum can stitch together life and death and heartbreak and hope and beauty and the past and the future. She is brilliant.

Dad knocks on the door softly.

"Noah, you look fantastic," he says. "What a suit. Now, may I have the pleasure of walking this fine family to the synagogue?"

I nod and my stomach flips and twists and turns because I have to go and do this now. My nerves spark up and down my skin.

We go down the stairs and out into the Saturday-morning sunlight, and the three of us walk to the synagogue. Dad talks about me flying to New York and taking me camping in the Catskills, which he says was his favourite ever thing to do – before work and the city got in the way. It sounds magic. He's asked me to stay before but it's never sounded like this.

Then we are there and my friends and the rest of our family are waiting.

I stand at the front and see their faces – Annie's is pale and serious, Mum's is flushed and delighted, Dad's is brushed with tears. And my nerves slip away just like the bird into the night.

I open my Torah and I read the story of when Noah sent a raven into the sky to see if there was a brand-new world somewhere out there.

Our books are tested
for children and young people by
children and young people.

Thanks to everyone who consulted on
a manuscript for their time and effort in
helping us to make our books better
for our readers.